Please look after this book and return it on time

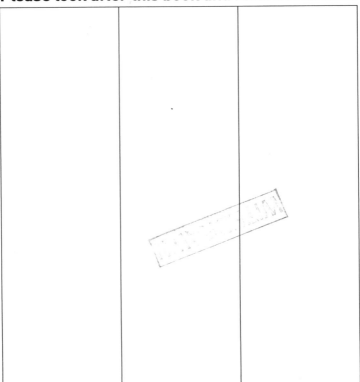

First published 2017 by Solaris
an imprint of Rebellion Publishing Ltd,
Riverside House, Osney Mead,
Oxford, OX2 0ES, UK

www.solarisbooks.com

ISBN: 978 1 78108 589 9

10 9 8 7 6 5 4 3 2 1

A CIP catalogue record for this book is available
from the British Library.

Designed & typeset by Rebellion Publishing

Printed in the UK

NEW YORK
THE RIVER THAT RUNS BOTH WAYS

Chapter One

CRUISING UP THE middle of the Hudson River a small boat filled with unlikely people rocks on the tide.

'These freaks are wiring their straps up to alarms now?' says God, shuffling in his sleep.

God is certainly an unlikely person, a man dressed in priest's robes, wearing a false beard that is held in place by a grubby elastic strap. He insists he's the God that Christians talk about, love, pray to and generally credit with the creation of all matter. He means this in a literal sense.

While he sleeps, his left foot is frequently tugged in different directions. This is because there is a baby tied to his big toe by a length of string. The baby is by no means a normal human baby—she has absolutely no intention of growing, she is far more interested in running around, diving in and out of the water and generally behaving with all the calm restraint of a happy kitten. God met the baby in Coney Island and has become rather attached to her. He means this in a figurative sense.

'What do you think he dreams about?' asks another of the boat's passengers. He's a young man known as Demi-John, a sideshow name for a sideshow performer. It is neither subtle nor, at first glance, inaccurate. There is, after all, only half of him. With deeper thought however, we realise the name's hardly fair. There is less of him than there is of us, yes. In fact, from the waist down there's nothing at all. But that is all of him. There is no other half of John, left kicking its heels (and little else) in a sideshow tent. Demi-John is one hundred percent John and he's perfectly comfortable with it, as should we be.

'I dread to think,' replies his friend, Peeper. Peeper is a beautiful girl, though perhaps not conventionally so. In a perfect world, none could fail to be moved by her warmth of spirit and gracious philosophy, but the world isn't perfect—especially now—and most folks are put off by the fact that her head is an enlarged eyeball and nothing else. 'I don't understand him when he's awake, never mind sleeping.'

'He's a good guy,' says Grace, the only passenger who could—if you were to insist on such a horribly exclusive term—pass for normal. Even then, being black, there are far too many times in the world's history where Grace would stand out. It just goes to show, appearances are nonsense. Grace is fifteen-years-old and is bobbing around on the Hudson in this mixed company because she's trying to find her brother, Brett. Last heard, Brett had been serving time on Rikers Island. Grace knows he's unlikely to still be there, so many months on from the world-changing events of The Change but she doesn't know where else to look. In a life of ill-fortune and general bad stuff, she's just glad that she's been lucky enough to find so many friends willing to help.

God is waking up and she wonders if his sleepy comment about straps offers a clue to his life pre-Change. Had he been a patient somewhere? The sort of patient that doesn't get out until the doctors say so? She decides she really doesn't care. She likes him and that's all that matters.

'God is very much a fan of breakfasts,' God announces, lapsing into the third person as he has a habit of doing when the mood takes him. 'What have we got?'

Grace digs around in one of the bags and pulls out a sandwich. God looks at it and decides that God won't complain today, God will just eat what he is given. He takes a large mouthful and breaks off a smaller piece for the baby who nearly takes off his thumb in her eagerness to get on the outside of some processed cheese and sourdough.

'Our first full day on the good ship *Baron Fabrizzi*,' God announces. It feels like the sort of thing that needs announcing, an important moment that should be spoken of ceremoniously. 'How did we all sleep?'

'Lousy,' says Peeper. 'Demi-John was throwing up for most of the night.'

'I didn't hear you,' God admits.

'It would have been hard over the noise of your snoring,' says Grace, not unkindly. 'You nearly choked on your beard a couple of times. Maybe you should strap it down at night.'

'Beards are unruly things,' God agrees. 'I sometimes wonder why I invented them. Perhaps I was feeling in an ornery mood that day. I think it was the fifth day, I was getting a bit twitchy by then. The first few days were plain sailing, all elephants and aardvarks and spaghetti Bolognese. Once I'd got stuck into all the complex stuff though, like jealousy and that weird feeling you have when you're heading for your plane and you know you've packed your passport but have to keep checking anyway... well, yes, by then things were getting on top of me.'

Nobody knows what to say to this so God finishes his sandwich in silence, offering the baby the crusts.

'Is it just me,' asks Demi-John, 'or is the Hudson longer than it used to be?' He looks out across the water, with a queasy look in his eyes. 'I mean, I thought it was only going to be a few miles you know? Not a huge expedition.'

'According to the Queen,' says Grace, by which she means the Queen of Coney Island, the changeable ruler of that stretch of theme parks and wildness, 'there are time bubbles.'

'Time bubbles,' says Peeper, 'you mentioned those. At the time I didn't like to ask, but...'

'What the hell are time bubbles?' finishes Demi-John.

Grace considers saying something wise and reassuring, then she decides it would be better to tell the truth. 'I didn't like to ask either.'

'Well obviously,' says God, 'I know exactly what they are.'

'Yeah?' asks Peeper.

'Naturally,' he brushes crumbs from his robes, 'they are bubbles in time.'

'Right,' says Demi-John, 'glad that's all cleared up.'

'They cause numerous strange effects,' God continues, 'including, but not limited to, making our journey seem a lot longer than it should.'

'Right.' Demi-John is all but certain there is little point in listening to the rest of this conversation.

'Imagine, if you will,' God continues, 'that you're walking along a road when all of a sudden you enter a time bubble and end up walking down the same stretch of road but at a different point in time. When you leave the bubble you have walked the same stretch of road twice, just at two different moments in its history. If you kept doing that, one bit of road would end up taking you a considerable time to walk along.'

'That actually makes sense,' says Grace.

'I'm glad you think so,' says God, 'personally I think inventing time was a huge mistake but there you go. You never have enough of it, people are always trying to steal some off you and it makes your body look horrible once you've had too much of it. Watches are so nice though, it seemed a waste not to give them something to do.' He looks at his naked wrist. 'I had a lovely watch once, it was a calculator too and played the theme tune to *Miami Vice* as an alarm. I miss that watch.'

The rest of the crew are spared asking what happened to this miraculous timepiece by something terribly distracting. It is the sort of something that very few people could ignore, even those deeply cursed with politeness, in order to maintain social graces and continue this discussion of timepieces. Even the most dedicated watch fan, someone who collects them and frequently wishes they owned many more wrists, would be forced to call time on the watch chat and address this new set of circumstances.

'Is it just me or did it suddenly become night time?' asks Peeper.

The sky around them is dark and filled with stars.

'It certainly looks like it,' agrees Demi-John.

'See?' says God. 'Time bubble. We're on the same stretch of water but at a different point in time. A point of time when it's night.'

'Great,' says Grace, 'because it was all too easy otherwise, wasn't it?'

On either side of them they can see the lights of the city, the Verrazano Bridge, running between Staten Island and Brooklyn, still further distant than it has any right to be.

'Maybe there's a way to navigate around them,' suggests God, 'shame we don't know it. Especially given that this time bubble is so unfriendly.'

'Unfriendly?' asks Grace.

God points behind them. 'Well, I don't want to pick favourites but I really don't like Nazis.'

'Nazis?' asks Peeper, staring at a dark shadow blotting out the stars behind them. It is the sort of dark shadow that those with an eye for such things would recognise as a submarine. 'What's a Nazi?'

'After your time,' he explains. 'One of those moments when a non-interventionist God takes a long hard look at the lovely walking mammals he's made and wonders if he should have added a pinch less free will. They torpedoed New York harbour during the Second World War.'

'There have been world wars?' Demi-John asks. '*Two* of them?'

'The first half of the twentieth century was a weird place to live,' God admits, 'almost as weird as the second half in fact.'

There is a whooshing sound and, in the distance, they can see a tanker momentarily lit up by an explosion.

The boat is a rough sketch of white light, translucent and insubstantial, existing only in the moment when the missile explodes. It is like a flashlight being shone on the history of ghosts.

'It had to be the Nazis,' God explains, 'who else would be floating around out here with all their lights off? I'd keep your heads down if I were you.'

Another torpedo cuts its way through the dark, and they lie face down on the deck of the *Baron Fabrizzi*, as, again, it brings a momentary daylight to the darkness of Lower Bay.

'Can they see us?' Demi-John asks.

'No lights,' says Grace, 'just keep down.'

'They're not going to be interested in a little boat like ours anyway,' God says. 'They're after the large tankers, the supply boats, the big targets. We just need to keep moving and hope we escape the bubble soon.'

Grace is at the wheel, trying to steer dead ahead while keeping her head down, painfully aware of how loud the engine sounds in the moments of calm between torpedoes.

God's baby is entranced by the explosions. It's a fireworks display she simply hasn't imagined could blow her own, innocent face off.

'Pam likes the explosions doesn't she?' God asks, having decided, quite on the spur of the moment, to name the baby.

The crew of the *Baron Fabrizzi* are suddenly aware of

the sound of German voices as a small searchlight sweeps the water.

'I think they've spotted us,' says Peeper.

'They should definitely put that light out,' says God.

There is the sudden, terrible noise of automatic rifle fire and Demi-John screaming.

'You alright?' Grace shouts, panicked. 'You hit?'

'No,' Demi-John replies. 'Just… I just panicked for a second, keep going!'

Grace doesn't need telling, she yanks the wheel one way and then the other, describing a zig-zag across the water, hoping to make them a less obvious target.

Suddenly there is a roar in the sky above them as a shell flies overhead, this time aimed at the U-Boat.

'Told them they shouldn't have turned on the light,' God says but nobody hears him as the shell hits, a funnel of water rising up and blotting out the stars before falling back down, its edges soaking them as their little boat rocks and spins in the aftershock. Pam is leaping up and down in glee; this has been *All the Fun*.

Suddenly it's daylight again and it's only their soaked clothes that prove they didn't dream the whole thing.

Chapter Two

'HOPEFULLY WE'LL AVOID too many bubbles like that,' says God after they've stripped down to their bare essentials, wrung out their clothes and draped them around the place to dry. As always, refusing in any way to suggest his beard is anything less than real, he has simply given it a thorough squeeze and it now sits like an exploding cloud across his face. 'But it could still takes us days just to get as far as the Narrows.'

'I really don't want to spend days on this boat,' says Demi-John and nobody disagrees with him. For one thing, they haven't got the supplies to last that long.

'Maybe if we go closer to the coast?' suggests Peeper. 'If these bubbles are only on the water then we might avoid them that way?'

'But we wouldn't avoid anything else,' Grace explains. 'The reason we're using the river is that things are so bad in those districts we'd never survive the trip.'

'We might not survive this one if we end up getting blown up by Nasties,' says Demi-John.

'Nazis,' God corrects him. 'Actually, no, forget it, you were right the first time.'

'For now,' Grace decides, 'I don't see we have much choice. We keep on going and hope we can somehow…'

The light changes again, becoming the soft, liquid light of dawn. On either side of them the city has vanished and the Verrazano Bridge is nowhere to be seen, a large sailing ship moored where one day it will be.

'Well,' says God, 'this is quite nice. Peaceful. A simpler time.'

'No Nasties?' Demi-John wonders, looking around them.

'Oh I think we're a few centuries away from all that,' says God. 'We should be fine.'

An arrow scythes past them into the water, landing with the sort of soft, gentle plop that can make you forget how absolutely not soft and gentle it would have felt had it been aimed a few inches either way.

In the distance, a shallow canoe of indigenous Americans is heading towards them.

'Why are they shooting at us?' asks Grace. 'We haven't even done anything!'

'Not yet, anyway,' God admits. 'Give them a few years and they might have due cause.'

'I don't think it's us they were aiming at,' says Demi-John, pointing at the water. A large grey shape breaks the surface, a puff of air from a puckered blowhole, and then vanishes again.

'Was it a manatee?' Grace asks, peering over the side. 'It looked too big to be a manatee.'

'Manatees,' explains God, 'do not have blowholes.'

'It looked like an elephant with flippers,' says Peeper. 'You think it wants to eat us?'

'I bet it wants to eat us,' Demi-John agrees.

'If it had wanted to eat us then it would have already taken a bite,' God suggests. 'Look at the size of it! We wouldn't cause it much trouble would we?'

In the distance, the hunters are shouting and paddling towards them. There's another volley of arrows, soaring high, whispering in the air and then raining into the water. A couple hit their target and the large creature rises up in a froth of white water. It is, as Peeper said, very much like an elephant who has decided to attend a fancy dress party as a fish. It has an extended, tentacle-like snout. Where an elephant would have thick, solid legs, this creature has wide, leaf-like flippers. Instead of flapping ears it has smooth, pulsating gills. Its soft, golden-coloured eyes are wide with fear and it roars with a strangely high-pitched, almost whale-like cry.

'It's beautiful!' says Peeper. 'Why are they trying to kill it?'

'They're hunters,' God tells her, 'they probably want to eat it.'

'Well,' she replies, watching as more arrows zip towards the creature, three more finding their mark, 'I don't want them to.'

She turns towards the hunter's boat and shouts at the top of her voice.

'Stop trying to kill the elephant fish! What's it ever done to you?'

There are many times in Peeper's life when she has had due cause to weep over her unusual appearance. The way people used to mock and gawp at her in the carnivals and sideshow tents, the way people would shout the most hurtful things as if a big eye meant she had a small heart. Today however, her appearance is a blessing. The hunters take one look at her, scream and begin paddling their boat in panicked retreat.

'That's right!' she shouts. 'And don't come back!'

The creature rises to the surface, its back bristling with arrows. It looks at them, they look back.

'It likes us,' says Peeper.

'It's an animal,' said God, 'it has no strong feelings either way. And this is coming from someone who loves all animals for obvious, egotistical reasons.'

'Yeah?' asks Peeper. 'Well, what's this one called then? As you created it, I'm sure you know.'

'Memory's a bit fuzzy,' God replies, 'I created a lot

you know. I've a feeling it's a Elefish. Or maybe an Aquatophant.'

'Kipsy,' says Grace, 'that's what it is, it's Kipsy.'

'Who's Kipsy?' asks Demi-John.

'There used to be loads of stories about a weird creature seen in the Hudson,' Grace explains. 'Most people figured they were just made up. They probably were. Like the Loch Ness monster or Yeti. Maybe that doesn't matter anymore. Since The Change even made up things are real.'

'I still think it likes us.' Peeper moves over to the side of the boat closest to the creature, holding out her hand in what she hopes is a suitably friendly gesture. 'It's alright,' she says, 'we don't want to hurt you, we like you. We think you're beautiful.'

Slowly, the creature extends its elongated snout and gives Peeper's hand a sniff. It must like what it finds because it glides over so that it's floating alongside the boat.

'Have we got anything we can feed her?' Peeper asks.

'Who says it's a her?' Demi-John asks but goes hunting in one of the packs until he finds a tin of fruit salad. 'You think Aquatiphants like fruit salad?'

'Of course!' says God, looking slightly jealously at the can. 'Who doesn't?'

Grace takes the can from Demi-John, opens it and offers it to Peeper. Peeper places the open mouth of the can beneath the creature's nose.

'Want some fruit salad?' she asks. 'It's nice.'

The creature takes a sniff, grabs the can with its trunk and throws the lot in its mouth.

'Not the can!' Peeper says. 'You can't eat that!'

She needn't worry, a second later the can is spat back at her, empty. Pam grabs it and plays it like a bongo drum.

'You think we should try and get the arrows out?' wonders Grace. 'It can't be good for her to just leave them like that, they might get infected.'

'I suppose we can try,' God agrees, 'though the minute you grab one it's likely to hurt, so be careful.'

'I'll do it,' says Peeper, stroking the creature, 'she trusts me I think.'

She bends down to look into its eyes. 'I'm going to help,' she says, 'it may hurt but sometimes things do, even though they're for the best.'

She takes the shaft of one of the arrows and pulls it free. The creature doesn't move. 'See,' says Peeper, holding the arrow up for it to see and sniff before throwing it into the boat, 'much better without it.'

She carefully removes the other arrows, holding each one up to the creature as she does so. Sometimes it shudders when they're removed, sometimes it sniffs their bloodied points, but it allows her to finish. At no time does it make quite so much of a fuss as Pam, who does a nervous stamp of her little feet each time an arrow is removed.

Once done, Peeper takes the empty fruit salad can back

from the baby and uses it as a cup to splash water on Kipsy's wounded back.

'They didn't go so deep,' says Peeper. 'She'll be just fine.'

'Let's hope we can say the same,' says God, pointing towards the sailing ship. 'I think we've been spotted.'

In the distance they can see the sailors looking out over the rail of the ship. The faint sound of shouting carries towards them on a gentle breeze.

'Is it us or Kipsy they're looking at?' Grace wonders. 'Either way we should probably get out of here.'

'If we can,' says Demi-John. 'Who knows how big this time bubble is? We could be stuck here for long enough that they'll catch us. What happens then? If we're caught here would we be stuck in this time? Or would we vanish the minute we left the river?'

'All good questions,' God admits, 'and I'm sure they have equally good answers. Let's just keep going and hope for the best, eh?'

'Maybe it wouldn't be so bad to be stuck here,' says Peeper. 'It's a nicer world than the one we left behind.'

'Looking like we do?' Demi-John says. 'Sorry Peeper, I'm not sure we'd go down very well here, look at the response you got from the hunters.'

'I certainly wouldn't have a nice life here,' says Grace, 'I'd end up on a slave ship.'

Kipsy gives a gentle bark and begins swimming downstream, moving at an angle to the distant ship. She halts again, gives another bark then continues, suddenly vanishing, the water sloshing in to fill the space she's left behind.

'Follow that Elefish!' says God. 'She's left the time bubble!'

Grace turns the wheel, aiming the *Baron Fabrizzi* at the point where Kipsy vanished. In the distance she's aware that the crew of the ship are lowering a rowing boat into the water, clearly intending to intercept them. If the exit from the bubble remains fixed, they'll be long gone before…

The light changes again and the city has returned on either side of them, the Narrows Bridge now much closer than it was before. Kipsy rolls in the water only a few feet away, offering up a cheerful howl before diving deeper and vanishing from sight.

'Is it just me or did Kipsy seem to know how to get home?' Grace asks. 'She found the exact place to swim, waited for us to watch and then… *poof!*'

'Animals are sensitive to things,' God agrees. 'Maybe she can see the time bubbles in a way we can't.'

'So,' says Peeper, 'we can follow her?'

'If we can find her again,' Demi-John is looking over the side of the boat, 'she's gone deep.'

'There she is!' Grace sees Kipsy's head bobbing up a few yards to their left and adjusts the wheel accordingly. 'Keep your eye on her, we'll follow her as far as we can.'

Weaving through the choppy Hudson, the *Baron Fabrizzi* and its passengers draw a strange line across the water. If viewed from above, their route would seem to suggest a drunk at the controls as they veer right and then left, then right again, following their guide as she avoids the time bubbles that are invisible to all except her.

The difference it makes to their progress is profound. Given the hours it has already taken them to cross a handful of miles, they're at the Narrows Bridge within a few minutes. If they'd gone straight it could have been days, maybe even years away. Not only have they avoided getting stuck in the time bubbles, they've used them to move faster, skipping through them like shortcuts.

'Kipsy's wonderful!' announces Peeper, clapping her hands.

'She gets my vote for skipper,' Demi-John agrees. 'In fact...' but nobody hears the rest of what he has to say as, with a clatter of chains, he's suddenly lifted off the deck of the boat entirely.

Chapter Three

IT'S NOT EASY feeding your family these days, Grimbo McClean thinks. Since The Change he's heard some claim that the greatest loss to civilisation is culture, others claim security, some even miss the government. For Grimbo, the only thing he really misses—with the possible exception of CBS on a long, dull night—is Glen's Deli and Mart. Life was just so much easier when you could get your groceries and smokes without breaking a sweat.

'God damn you Johnnie, get that kink out of your chain!' he shouts at his son. 'It'll catch when you yank her in otherwise and then I'll be down there fishing *you* out rather than dinner.'

Johnnie mumbles an apology. Soft ass kid is always apologising for something, Grimbo thinks. Walks around as if the world owes him a favour. Should take a long hard look at the state of the city and wonder how he's doing compared to most. They eat regularly enough, there's always plenty to be found in the river, even these days.

Bob McCannick came up with the idea that they could fish for their supper, dangle their hooks off the Narrows Bridge and see what they could find. Always was a good old boy was Bob. Shame he had to go the way he did but that's democracy for you; he shouldn't have suggested fishing if he was going to get cold feet at what they caught. There are twenty hungry folks in the gang and they're not going to go hungry just because someone gets picky about species. They fish for anything with a pulse. That's just, *whatdoyoucallit*, survival of the fittest. That's man rising up against his challenges and Making Things Work.

Bob hadn't seen it that way.

The day Grimbo had caught that young student on his hook, all beaded hair and tattoos, Bob had kicked up a stink saying she weren't the sort of thing they should be fishing for. Well, Grimbo had been inclined to disagree. In fact, Grimbo had disagreed with the tip of his gaff and that was two fish for the pot. Bob hadn't been good eating, too damn old and skinny, but the student had made up for it. He'd wondered if her tattoos would be poisonous but then remembered that those Japanese used to serve up squid with ink. Hadn't done them any harm. Probably. He'd expected them to taste sort of metallic, like when you chewed the end of a ballpoint and it squirted in your mouth. Turned out they hadn't tasted at all.

The Fishermen had thrived after that. There was always something stupid sailing up the Hudson, thinking it was a free ride into the city. Well, the Fishermen were the toll and very pleased to see you thank you very much!

'I've got one!' shouts Johnnie.

This is surprising to Grimbo on two levels. Firstly: he hadn't even seen anything coming up the river. A while ago, there had been a small boat a distance away but it had vanished into one of the soft places. Grimbo knew all about the soft places, you went in and then you were some other *when* entirely. Sometimes you didn't come out.

The second thing that surprises Grimbo is that his son has never caught a damn thing. In fact, he's always thought the little snot made a point of avoiding it. The kid's happy enough to eat what they catch, but too much of a wuss to do any of the catching. Grimbo had made him use a gaff on a guy they'd fished out of an inflatable dinghy once, by way of a life lesson. It had been hard to tell which one of them had been crying harder, the kid or the fish. 'Just smack it hard here!' he'd told the kid, poking the crying dinghy-fish in the eye. 'One good whack and it's all done but the frying.'

In the end the kid had made a mess of the fish's face: two shallow cuts to the forehead and a punctured cheek. Grimbo had had to finish the job off himself, he couldn't stand making an animal suffer like that. He'd decided there was really no hope for little Johnnie. No sir, no hope at all. But now he's caught something. Could be he's done the kid a disservice.

'What have you got big fella?' he asks, giving the kid a dose of upbeat. "Ain't you the bestest little son of a bitch?" tone of voice, just to show he can be nice when given due cause. "Live life by the stick and the carrot," as his old man used to say before the emphysema stopped him saying any damn thing at all.

'Some guy,' Johnnie replies.

'Some guy, he says!' Grimbo pats Johnnie on the back, trying not to sneer in disgust as this nearly knocks the kid over. 'Let's have a look.'

Grimbo grabs the kid's chain and gives it a yank, pleased by the sound of screaming and panic from below; they'd got this fish hooked good and it sounded like there were more waiting to jump on. 'Get those hooks swinging, boys!' he shouts to the other Fishermen on duty. 'We've got a shoal!'

He peeks over the edge of the bridge, being real careful. Sometimes the fish shoot at them so you have to mind yourself. It's the same little boat he saw earlier, he's sure of it. Three weirdoes, a black kid and a baby. He briefly wonders if they're anything to do with the Queen of Coney Island; he has a kind of agreement with her, after she threatened to get nasty. He leaves her lot alone and she leaves him alone. That, my friends, is what you call civilisation. He thinks about it for a minute, he doesn't want to cause trouble but he's also mighty hungry and this is enough to keep them fed for days. The baby's a real draw too. They've had baby once before and it was as sweet and soft as a pretty little meat cake. He decides that this don't look like any of her folks and that he'll swear to that should it come back to bite him on the ass.

'They're going under the bridge!' shouts Ike, from behind Grimbo. 'How did they sneak up on us so fast?'

Ike's one of his best men, probably the only one who can hook a fish like Grimbo can. He don't look like much: five and a half feet, light build. Pre-Change he managed one of those Mammon Burger joints, the places that used to do the little fried jalapenos and the barbecue-seasoned fries. Grimbo used to love going to Mammon Burger.

'Soft places,' Grimbo says, pulling on Johnnie's chain. 'Popped out of one right below us. They can't hide under there forever. Besides, we got one of 'em here!'

Chapter Four

DEMI-JOHN IS LUCKY about one thing: the hook has caught in the strap of his bib pants, not his flesh. If it had hooked into the meat of his back he would have been horrifically wounded with each sharp tug. As it is, he really only has to worry about the fact that he's being drawn further and further from the boat. To begin with, he tries to reach around and unhook himself. Once he's been pulled a decent height above the deck of the *Baron Fabrizzi* though, he stops doing that. This far up, the last thing he wants is for the hook to slip; in fact he's praying it holds, if he fell into the water from this height he'd be dead for sure.

More chains are dropping on either side, swinging through the air at speed, their shining metal hooks glinting as they scythe towards his friends, hoping to catch a bite.

He watches them duck and panic, sees God pull Pam to safety under his robes and shout at Grace. He's telling her to get the boat under the bridge so they have cover. He wonders if they'll abandon him. He supposes they might not have a choice.

As he reaches the roadbed of the bridge, hands grab at him and one of the Fishermen yanks him up. Demi-John gets a good look at them. They're a rough lot, dressed in dirty, mismatched clothes. They look like the sort of people you normally find sleeping under bridges rather than fishing off them.

'Where's the rest of it?' one of them asks. 'Its legs just fall off or something?'

'This is all of me,' he tells them with a big smile, hoping— stupidly, he knows—that he might be able to charm his way out of whatever situation this is he's fallen into.

'Damn it sideways!' another shouts. 'Legs and rump are the best part.'

Rump? Demi-John thinks. Rump as in steak? "Rump" is not a word he wants to hear right now. For the first time in his young life he's rather glad he doesn't own one.

'You think I should throw it back?' asks the man who's holding his chain. The look on this man's face makes it perfectly clear that there is only one correct answer to this question. 'You saying my kid's first catch isn't good enough for you? You saying he was supposed to know the fish didn't have no legs?'

'I ain't saying nothing like that Grimbo,' says the fan of rump, 'your kid did good. Just like a bit of rump is all.'

'Pete, one more word out of you and I will kick you so hard in *your* rump that your hipbones jump up and smash you in your ugly face,' says Grimbo, holding Demi-John up by the scruff of his neck and unhooking him. 'You hear me?'

'I hear you Grimbo, it ain't no big thing OK? I'm just saying…'

Grimbo doesn't want to hear what Pete's saying. He drops Demi-John to the floor—*Hell*, he thinks, *what's it going to do? Run off?*—and charges at Pete, meaning to do some damage.

The other Fishermen, still swinging their chains and hooks, turn towards the fight. Some of them even let go of their chains and make to come over. Grimbo doesn't take kindly to this; Grimbo isn't in a mood to take kindly to anything.

'You get back on your hooks, damn you!' he shouts as he grabs Pete by the throat.

'Jesus Grimbo!' Pete's shouting, in the sort of way a man does when he really wants to keep all his teeth. 'There ain't no need for…'

Pete's flying. Grimbo has thrown him off the edge of the bridge so he can offer his final explanations to the sixty odd yards of thin air between him and the Hudson River. He doesn't bother, just screams in a manner that starts off as frustration and ends up at panic. Grimbo watches him go, watches him do his best to turn his freefall into a dive.

'Hey Ike,' Grimbo asks, 'you know stuff. What's the highest anyone took a dive from?'

'And lived?' Ike asks.

'Yeah,' Grimbo agrees, 'and lived.'

'Not this high,' Ike tells him.

'Thought not.' Grimbo nods as Pete hits the river. He wonders what he broke on the way in. Fingers for sure, arms probably, maybe he even cracked open his skull. There's no way of knowing as Pete never surfaces again.

'I guess that was a waste,' he admits, only now getting his temper under control. 'I probably shouldn't have done that.'

'Dad?'

He turns to see Johnnie looking panicked. What's wrong with the kid now? Got himself all torn up because he had to watch daddy throw an idiot into the river?

'What's the problem, son?' he asks. 'You don't like me standing up for you?' Maybe, now he thinks about it, he would have been better throwing Johnnie in the river. At least Pete had been able to fish. Still, his wife wouldn't have liked it and he gets enough grief from her as it is. Sometimes he thinks he should just keep her in that damn crate all the time, she's just too unruly when he lets her out.

'The fish, dad,' says Johnnie, pointing at the bridge railing. 'He ran away.'

'Ran away? How the hell can he have ran away? He didn't have no legs!'

He runs to the edge of the bridge and looks over just in time to see Demi-John swinging into the gaps in the bridge construction. Below the road surface there's a criss-crossed sandwich of metal struts and support beams, the damned no-leg freak has pulled himself inside it and there's no easy way to get him back out.

On the one hand, Grimbo knows it ain't worth the effort, on the other he knows that to let the fish escape won't look good in front of the others. He supposes he's just going to have to go down there and fetch him back out. The politics of leadership are a bitch.

'You could have tried to stop him,' he tells Johnnie, giving him a slap to the head. 'I ought to make *you* go down there and get him.'

The look of fear on Johnnie's face is so strong Grimbo feels his breakfast rising back up. 'Ah to hell with you,' he says, 'you'd only screw it up and then I'd have to fetch you both out.'

He turns to the rest of the Fishermen. 'If one of you hasn't caught something by the time I get back, I've a good mind to throw you *all* in after Pete.'

He'd have a hard time managing it, he knows, but he's thinking of that carrot and stick his old man liked to talk about again.

'Goddamnit,' he says to himself, stepping out over the edge of the bridge and lowering himself, carefully, to the hidey-hole below it.

'WHAT DO WE do?' asks Peeper, holding her hands over her shiny head, trying not to think what would happen if one of these swinging hooks were to imbed itself in it.

At God's instruction, Grace has cut the engine, dropping their anchor so that they're now directly below the bridge, for all the good it does them. The Fishermen may not be able to see them but it's not stopping them whirling their hooks blindly.

They heard—but were too busy ducking to really see— Pete take a dive. For a moment they thought it might have been their friend but a quick glance put their minds at rest on that.

'We've got to get Demi-John back,' Grace says. 'We need to catch the hooks.'

'We need to what?' Peeper is not entirely down with this idea.

God is slowly nodding, a big, mad smile on his face. 'I like your style,' he tells Grace. 'Do a bit of fishing ourselves?'

'Exactly,' Grace agrees, 'but we'll have to do it carefully and quickly.'

She looks around, a hook passing so close to her face that she actually feels the air move between its tip and her nose. She spots a blanket, grabs it and waits for her chance.

UNDERNEATH THE BRIDGE, Demi-John is surprised to find that for once he has the advantage. His arms are stronger than most people's—they have to be, they do the hard work—and he can swing and climb between the metal struts with ease. Now his only problem is what to do now he's down here. It's still too far to jump. Maybe... *maybe*, if he can make it to one of the supporting pillars he could climb down it. From this far back he can't tell. Is the concrete flush? A solid drop all the way down? Or will there be handholds, some way of getting down the slow way, the way that doesn't break your neck?

If he does manage that, he might be able to get back to the *Baron Fabrizzi*.

'Hey!' he shouts, trying to get their attention, 'I'm up here!'

'Not for long, fish,' says a voice from behind him and he can see one of the Fisherman, the leader no less, climbing after him. How long can he avoid him under here? Certainly not long enough that he might be able to escape. As the only alternative is to allow himself to be dragged back up to the surface, he doesn't see he has much choice so begins moving faster, aiming for the support pillar.

'I've caught something!' shouts Ike.

'Me too,' says Paulie, a rather rotund guy who gets a lot of flak for always being in the front of the line at mealtimes. 'I can't seem to shift it though, it's holding fast.'

'Same,' Ike agrees.

'I'm biting!' shouts another of the Fishermen, a sullen, unfriendly guy called Scott that nobody really likes.

'And me,' cries the last Fisherman, Old Bob, who has strong arms but weak teeth. Old Bob has to suck his fish.

Johnnie has given up on fishing. He watches the other four men as they continue to tug and swear at their lines. Underneath the bridge he can hear his Dad shouting his usual threats and big talk. Johnnie comes to a decision. He walks off the bridge, never looks back, never goes back. Some people say family is everything but he just never did like his much.

'Look,' says Peeper, 'it's John!'

Looking up, Grace and God can see their friend as he swings beneath the bridge, aiming for one of the taught chains.

'He'll have to be quick,' says Grace.

'None quicker,' says Peeper.

DEMI-JOHN CAN SEE what his friends are doing—they've caught the other end of the Fishermen's chains and have hooked them onto parts of the boat. Now, as much as the Fishermen tug, they can't lift what they've caught. Will they give up on their chains and hooks or will they keep tugging, blind to what they're attached to? He decides they can do what they like as long as they give him long enough to use one of the chains to his advantage.

He swings from one of the support struts onto the closest chain, dropping down it as quickly as he can, hand over hand.

'Let go!' Grimbo shouts above him. 'Let go of the chains you idiots!'

'CAN YOU HEAR Grimbo?' Paulie wonders.

'Say what?' asks Old Bob who hasn't heard anything clearly since Bush was in the White House.

'I thought I heard Grimbo shouting to let go of the chains,' Paulie clarifies.

'Probably talking to that no-legged son of a bitch,' reckons Old Bob. 'He wouldn't want us to let go would he? Not while we've got a hold of something.'

'Guess not,' Paulie agrees. 'Sure is putting up a hell of a fight though.'

Ike has wound the chain around his forearms. He's turned away from the edge of the bridge and is using his legs to brace himself against the barrier. 'I'm going to get this fish landed,' he says through gritted teeth, putting all of his weight onto the line. 'Just see if I don't.'

Scott's not convinced. 'Whole thing stinks if you ask me.'

But they didn't ask him, they don't like him and they're all only too happy to ignore him.

'LET GO OF the damned chains!' Grimbo is screaming. Why is he the only one around here with a brain? He grabs the chain the escaping fish is climbing down and gives it a good shake, determined to make him loose his grip.

'I'VE GOT IT in on the run!' Paulie screams. 'It's thrashing around like a worm on a hotplate!'

'We haven't got a hotplate, Paulie!' Bob shouts, his dumb, deaf ears missing most of what's going on. 'We'll just have to barbecue 'em like normal.'

*   *   *

THE CHAIN DANCING around in his grip, Demi-John drops the last few feet into the water and swims to the boat.

'Go!' God shouts as he drags his friend back onboard, but Grace doesn't need telling, she's lifted the anchor, started the engine and revving it for all its worth.

The *Baron Fabrizzi* shoots north, coming out of the other side of the Narrows bridge, the four chains still attached.

Underneath the bridge, Grimbo loses his balance as the chain snaps towards him. Falling, he grabs the only thing he can reach, the one thing that won't help him: the chain itself. He has a moment to make brief eye contact with Paulie, who's been pulled from the bridge, the chain still in his hands as they both fall towards the river, the chain becoming slack between them.

That miserable bastard is looking at me as if it's my fault, Paulie thinks, just before he hits the surface of the Hudson and his spine is shattered into pieces as small as dice.

Ike backflips over the bridge. *What the hell are those?* he wonders as a pair of red spheres bristling with white shards swoop into his vision. He realises they're his own shattered knees.

'Those are my goddamned knees!' he shouts to Scott, who is sailing through the air towards him as if planning on racing him to the finish line below.

'God damn it!' Old Bob shouts, letting go of his chain as

it bites into his hands. The chain whips away and vanishes over the edge of the bridge. 'Would you just look at that?' He looks around. 'Fellas?' He stands up, his legs aching from having been sat too long. 'Fellas?' He's all on his own up there. 'Now just where in Sam Hill have you all run off to?' he wonders.

Chapter Five

GRACIE FFORDE IS not having a "get things done" kind of day.

You would hope, being one of the few people left with some kind of power and authority in a world where chaos is the norm, that one could expect each day to bring at least *something* positive. *It's not like I'm greedy*, she thought—though she was, mercilessly, voraciously, hatefully greedy—*I know it's not like the old days when you could destroy an entire multinational corporation before brunch. I'm not expecting miracles. Just a little sign that the world is still spinning my way.*

Gracie is a member of The Hellfire Club, a small collection of fortunate individuals who have weathered The Change if not entirely—you can't have an extinction event without breaking some eggs—then at least favourably. They have retained assets in the form of belongings, people, technology, weapons, food... They are, for want of a better word, a ruling class here in the rubble of the post-Change world.

Gracie made her original fortune in food retail. A line of supposedly healthy microwave meals that had appealed to the gym and squash set willing to pay the exorbitant mark-up on what was, after all, nothing more exciting than a small bucket of plastic filled with reconstituted chicken, monosodium glutamate and enough salt to give a cod cottonmouth. Gracie had understood the first rule of food retail: to hell with what you put in, as long as it sounds like the right things were taken out. Artificial preservatives, sugar, colouring... The more you could claim your food lacked, the more people would pay top dollar to consume it. From that initial success she had gone on to make money from everything and anything she could lay her hands on. Chiefly, in those last halcyon days before the world fell on its ass and refused to get back up, arms.

To some the transition from food retail to smart bombs might seem bizarre and random but, as Grace was always quick to point out when asked at the sort of thousand dollar a plate parties she had often attended, there was a common thread: money. You could make a fortune out of either and that's all she really cared about.

True, in the months since The Change, she'd had

44

multiple opportunities to thank her lucky stars that her business interests had veered in the way they had. As a highly successful owner of an arms manufacturing company she'd been well-placed to survive the events that had killed so many others. Gracie Fforde wouldn't have retained the position she currently did if she'd been able to meet the apocalypse with nothing more potent than a low-carb turkey lasagne. As the owner of several local warehouses, packed to the rafters with assorted machinery designed to eradicate people in inventive and technologically impressive ways, she'd been a dead cert for success in this new, fractured age.

She didn't sell her weaponry anymore of course, that would be pointless. What could people give her that she couldn't already take? She used it as leverage. This was a dangerous world and the person that held the biggest gun held the greatest power. She had even managed to conscript entire districts to her service via the simple, yet effective, method of walling off small areas and then placing a high-yield explosive at the centre of them; if her tenants did as they were told the bomb would never be triggered. They would work for Gracie—and would be fed in return, she wasn't completely without compassion—and the bomb could gather dust, safe and sound as a deterrent. It had worked for world powers for decades; she could hardly claim to have invented the idea, but it all helped ensure that, unlike most, Gracie

Fforde had done quite well out of the end of the world.

But not today.

'Is that even a boat?' she asks her PA, Gordon Monitor. Mr Monitor is a very precise man. She has no idea where he finds hair wax these days and can only assume he has an entire wardrobe of identical navy blue suits to allow him to appear so disgustingly tidy at all times.

'Once,' he replies, 'it was probably a very nice boat. Now we should kill it with fire.'

Gracie can't help but agree. She's been waiting here on a Staten Island pier for several hours, eager to greet a shipment of a new drug. The drug is called chase, invented—or rather discovered—by another member of The Hellfire Club, an oily little Brit called Milo Shandler. He had found considerable success using the drug as a method of controlling people. It was highly addictive but not particularly debilitating, so the hooked little junkies could still work, willing to do whatever it took for the next snort of chase. It was a dried leaf and a lovely big bale of it was supposed to be on the boat they were here to meet. *This* boat. This boat that now appears to be nothing less than a floating, writhing somewhat angry bush.

'Mr Shandler mentioned some issues with sproutlings,' says Monitor, 'users being converted into animated vegetable matter?'

'Yes,' says Gracie, 'he did.'

'Looks to me like the problem is even more profound than he suggested.'

'Yes,' says Gracie, 'it does.' She looks to one of her men, a lumpen pile of muscle and steroid injections who is all but splitting his Coast Guard uniform. 'I would very much like you to destroy that boat now,' she says, 'before it gets any closer and contaminates all of us.'

'Ma'am,' he agrees, nodding so hard his baseball cap nearly falls off.

'What's your name?' she asks.

'Ollie Brake,' he replies, flattered to have been asked.

'Mr Brake, I'm going to need you to destroy that boat both thoroughly and yet extremely carefully.'

'Yes ma'am.'

'I want you to look at that boat and imagine you are staring right into the leafy jaws of something that could do us all some terrible, lasting harm. Because, make no mistake, that's precisely what you are doing. If that thing's infectious, and we must assume it is, then we need to ensure every single leaf is burned and disposed of with no contamination whatsoever.'

'Yes ma'am.'

'I'm glad we understand each other Mr... What's your name?'

'Ollie Brake, ma'am.' He is less flattered now it's become clear she can forget the information in a matter of seconds.

'See to it now Mr Brake.'

'Sure thing ma'am.' Gracie watches him walk away. 'Do you think we can trust him to do the job properly Mr Monitor?'

'I would hope so, ma'am,' Gordon replies. 'It is, after all, his life on the line as much as ours.'

'This is true, that sort of thing can be very motivational for people like… What was his name Mr Monitor?'

'I don't believe I caught it ma'am. Would you like me to put through a call to Mr Shandler again? We should explain what has happened to his delivery.'

'Let me tell you something Mr Monitor.'

'Yes ma'am?'

'Mr Shandler could spend the next five years cleaning my shoes with his tongue and I would still not give him the time of day.'

'Yes ma'am.'

'He could, in fact, act as my own personal, walking toilet and yet I would not trouble to look him in the eye, however competently, however lip-smackingly he performed the duty.'

'No ma'am.'

'In short Mr Monitor, Milo Shandler is dead to me.'

'Yes ma'am.'

'Kindly don't trouble my ears with the sound of his name ever again.'

'I won't ma'am.'

'Mr Monitor?'

'Yes ma'am?'

'Is it just me or can you see another boat approaching?'

THE BOAT IN question is the *Baron Fabrizzi* and its crew are still far too relieved about their escape from the Fishermen to have noticed they are sailing into danger.

They have unhooked the chains, listened to Demi-John's breathless account of being chased by a loon and settled back in the hope of a few minutes of enjoyable boredom. Needless to say, a few minutes would be all they would manage.

It's Milo Shandler's boat bursting into flames that really draws their attention. How could it not? Even when you're trying your very best to not notice anything that might turn your trip from idle to adventurous, it's hard to gloss over a pillar of flame and screeching plantlife stretching forty feet into the air.

'That's a big fire,' comments Demi-John.

'We should keep as far away as we can,' God suggests, 'let them get on with setting fire to things in a really big and scary manner while we just, you know, go away as fast as possible.'

Grace nods, steering the *Baron Fabrizzi* towards the Brooklyn side of the Narrows, keeping as much distance between them and the conflagration as she can.

*　　*　　*

GRACIE IS ENJOYING the sight of the burning boat—as much as she can be said to enjoy anything. Ms Fforde is not a woman entirely comfortable with the notion of pleasure. She has found that by imagining Milo Shandler himself to be onboard, popping and bubbling in the extreme heat, his sanctimonious smile burned right off his stupid, stupid face, the sight is even more edifying. She momentarily considers calling Shandler, despite her snotty dismissal of the idea when Mr Monitor suggested it. She could call him, point the camera at the blazing boat and then tell him he'll get his soon enough. Then she'd hang up while he quaked in his prissy little loafers.

She doesn't do this because:

a) She feels she really needs to work on her negativity issues, and

b) Having told Mr Monitor she doesn't want the name Milo Shandler being brought up she fears she'll look really pathetic if she now does so.

Never look pathetic in front of your staff, they're probably laughing at you most of the time anyway, they don't need an extra excuse.

She decides the new boat on the river will provide a welcome distraction.

'Do we know the people on that boat?' she asks Mr Monitor.

'I don't believe so,' he says, handing her a small pair of binoculars.

She looks through them and is heard to give a tiny exhalation of disgust. 'Mr Monitor, that is not the sort of boat I want sailing on my river,' she says. 'It's being driven by a black keeping company with two freaks and a pervert in a pretend beard.'

'I'm disgusted, ma'am,' Mr Monitor replies, sounding nothing of the sort. Mr Monitor, like his employer, is not one for overt expressions of emotion.

'Just the sort of people any decent extinction event should have disposed of,' she says.

'Indeed,' he agrees.

'This, of course, is the problem with The Change,' she continues, warming to just above absolute zero. 'Many of those who survived were the layabouts, the wasters. The people lying around in bed at that time in the morning.'

'Absolutely,' says Mr Monitor, very sensibly not pointing out that their mutual survival might be seen to put them in the same bracket.

'We lost the real grafters,' she continues, 'the lifeblood of the economy. We are forced, once again, to try and build a decent society on foundations of cheap clay. We can only do the best we can. *Be* the very best we can.'

'Inspirational,' he replies, feeling it's time for a bit of calm devotion.

'Thank you Mr Monitor, I try to be. It's what God would

have wanted. Now send a Coast Guard patrol over there to shoot those horrible people dead.'

'Immediately, ma'am.'

Chapter Six

IT'S WHAT GOD *would have wanted.*

If Gracie Fforde had only known the passenger list of the small boat in question, she could have gone straight to the horse's mouth and checked. She would have found that God most certainly didn't want to be shot. In fact, if asked at that very moment, God would have admitted that what he really wanted was some onion rings, had been hankering after some in fact ever since waking up. It just goes to show, even deities can remain unfulfilled in this modern age.

'Oh,' Grace sighs, noticing the Coast Guard boat bobbing towards them. It curves around the still-flaming ruin of Shandler's boat; dark ash cinders, holding the vague form of leaves, rising up from it like Chinese sky lanterns, breaking up on the breeze. 'This can't be good.'

'Can we go faster?' Peeper asks.

'In this thing?' Grace shakes her head. 'We'd have more chance of outrunning them if we got out and walked.'

'Maybe they just want to talk?' God says. 'We can't just always assume the worst. I refuse to believe that the vast majority of my glorious human race are now a bunch of psychotic assholes.'

A sweet thought, a father resolutely proud of his noble children. It's a shame that the coast guard choose that moment to start shooting at the boat as the gunfire does rather take the edge off his sentiment.

'Psychotic assholes!' God shouts falling back into the boat, causing Pam to emerge from underneath his robes where she had eventually fallen asleep. She runs towards the prow of the boat, yanking his leg after her. 'Get down crazy baby!' he shouts, trying to return his leg to the safe cover of the boat before someone is unkind enough to shoot it off.

But Pam is not to be calmed. The bullets continue to litter a perfectly pleasant New York morning and she wants none of it. She is, not to put too fine a point on it, livid about them.

'Woah!' God is dragged across the deck of the boat as Pam, with the sort of strength and energy one would really not expect from a baby, leaps across the deck, dragging him behind her as if he weighs nothing.

'Hang on!' Grace shouts.

'I'd never have thought of that!' God cries, his feet

slamming into the prow of the boat as Peeper and Demi-John dash to help.

'My toe's coming off!' God shouts, grabbing the string that attaches him to Pam to relieve the strain. Peeper and Demi-John grab hold too, all three of them bracing themselves against the side of the boat.

'Come back Pam!' he shouts. 'You're a terribly naughty baby.'

She doesn't but surely, with all three of them holding on, she won't be able to get far? She's jumped into the water just ahead of the boat, surely it will mow her down any moment? That's not what happens, what happens is that the *Baron Fabrizzi* suddenly picks up speed, dragged along by the absurd pull of the baby who is now doing a doggy paddle so vigorous, passing fish must surely be pausing in their business of swimming simply to watch in awe.

'Well, now,' says God, bullets accompanying them like fat flies in summer as they begin to cruise away at top speed, 'this is a thing isn't it?'

IN THE WATER, the initial panic of being shot at is all but forgotten as Pam feels water rush by. The simple truth of it is: life is just too much fun to worry for long, the joy of swimming as fast and as hard as she can is so invigorating, so utterly, utterly brilliant that she's laughing at the top of her small voice, the sound escaping in a small trail of bubbles that ripple behind her. She's never felt more alive, more perfect, more herself. She wonders if she can just swim all the way around the world and back. She thinks she probably could. In fact she thinks she could probably do anything.

'Is THAT BOAT a speedboat, Mr Monitor?' asks Gracie Fforde, quite beside herself with revulsion at yet another example of the world not doing the things she wants it to.

'It appears to be being powered by a baby, ma'am,' Mr Monitor replies, utterly aware of how awful and ridiculous the words are in his mouth.

'That's just...' Ms Fforde is almost, almost lost for words. 'It's really not acceptable, is it, Mr Monitor?'

'No ma'am, it most certainly isn't.'

'A baby?'

'I know, ma'am.'

'I worry about the state of the world today Mr Monitor, I worry a great deal.'

Mr Monitor is not an idiot. He is aware he works for someone that might occasionally appear to be. He has given some thought to this because Mr Monitor is a very thoughtful man. By which we mean he thinks a lot. He is certainly not thoughtful in the sense he is ever considerate to others. On the subject of his employer's intelligence he has come to a number of conclusions. Like all rich idiots, his employer's idiocy is specific to a number of areas, areas that—fortunately for his employer—have never impinged on her ability to make a great deal of money. When it comes to that, to the stockpiling of obscene amounts of cash, she is as far from being an idiot as a subway train is from being a fish. Where her idiocy comes into play, where it really begins to *shine*, is in her worldview. Given that, temporally speaking, they are currently standing on the more uncomfortable side of a global extinction event, statements such as the one she has just made, claiming to worry about the state of the world, are so stupid as to seem like the utterings of an imbecile. It is the sort of statement that would have a lazy writer reaching for the adjective "blithering" when wanting to thoroughly qualify her idiocy to their readers (as if they would need help in that regard). This is because, Mr Monitor has decided, and who are we to argue, that people like Ms Fforde simply cannot see the world, nor indeed any of the people in it, properly. This is because they do not really understand what it is to be human. This is because they spend too much time dealing in the aforementioned obscene piles of cash and not enough doing anything else. Mr Monitor is of the opinion that his employer is what used to be, unpleasantly and insultingly, referred to as an "idiot savant". Someone with mental difficulties who could, nonetheless, utterly excel in certain focused directions.

Simply: she sucks at everything expect moolah.

But, as previously made only too clear, Mr Monitor is not an idiot, and only an idiot would share this opinion with their employer.

'It is extremely worrying, ma'am,' Mr Monitor agrees.

'As you may know, Mr Monitor,' Ms Fforde continues, because the depths of her selective idiocy have not quite been plumbed, 'I am a great believer in the rights of babies.'

'I was not aware of that, ma'am,' he replies.

It has taken him a fraction of a second to decide on this route. On the one hand, he likes to be seen to know her every whim. On the other, people do like to express new opinions without being seen to repeat themselves. The latter opportunity seemed too good to miss. It is quick-thinking like this that has allowed Mr Monitor to not only continue existing post-Change but also thrive.

'Oh indeed, Mr Monitor, it is a subject very dear to me. I once donated money to a pro-life charity for that very reason.' Which is true, though she had misheard the man who had been asking for money, thinking she was tipping him for parking her car. Once the penny had dropped—*Oh my, but this attendant does bang on about foetuses*, she had thought for thirty confused seconds—she had decided to let him keep the money in case anybody was watching. Though what he hoped to achieve with her five dollars had always been quite beyond her. 'That said, babies like *that.* Ones who drag boats around the Hudson like a child's toy, a child's toy filled with freaks and a black…'

She's losing her thread. Mr Monitor is quick to nudge her back on track: 'Yes, ma'am, *those* sorts of babies?'

'Well, they are deserving of no rights at all,' she finishes, secretly a bit upset that the sentence hasn't finished with quite as much creative venom as she'd been hoping for.

'Well,' says Mr Monitor, only too aware of his employer's needs and willing to fulfil them, 'one can only hope the Coast Guard will manage to shoot it in a flurry of watery offal.'

'Oh indeed, Mr Monitor,' Ms Fforde purrs.

BUT THE COAST Guard are struggling to do anything of the sort. Grace might like to take some credit thanks to her hard work at the wheel but in truth all she's doing is holding onto the thing and being flung whichever way the rudder forces her. Pam is entirely to blame for their continued survival as she dips and swerves from one side of the river to the other, their pursuers simply unable to second-guess the direction the boat will take next as it is so chaotic, so ridiculous that they are having to console themselves by swearing loudly and shooting at fresh air.

After sixty seconds or so of this, the guards are putting a show on for their employers and have entirely given up on achieving their homicidal aim. Shooting a boat of strange people being towed by a baby quite simply takes more effort than *appearing* to shoot a boat of people being towed by a baby. This is why, after that initial, potentially fatal minute, Grace and her friends are more or less safe; they are not so much being hunted as taking part in a water-based art installation involving machine guns and rude words.

And then, as they approach the waters of the Upper Bay, something particularly surprising happens: the Coast Guard simply stop firing, turn their boat around and head back towards the still flaming remains of Milo Shandler's boat. The timing is perfect as Pam, having attacked the river at full throttle is finally tiring. She sways out in an arc next to the boat and God, Peeper and Demi-John fish her back in. She crawls onto God's lap and instantly falls asleep. Grace cuts the engine and they slowly approach relative stillness, bobbing on the water, not a little travel sick and confused.

'Why did they just stop shooting at us?' Grace asks, knowing nobody is going to be able to give her a good answer.

'I'm not complaining,' says God. He's untied Pam from his big toe, thankful to still have it attached and not willing to risk losing it next time. He loops the string around a wooden bracket on the boat instead.

'Maybe they don't have any authority on this stretch of the river?' suggests Peeper.

'They didn't look like the sort of people who worried about authority,' says Demi-John, 'and with amazing guns like that why would they?'

'Guns are never amazing,' says God, 'they just fling bits of metal into people which is a stupid and horrible thing to do. I would never have created guns. It takes a real lunatic to invent something as pointless and ugly as a gun.'

'Someone woke up terribly preachy this morning,' mutters Demi-John.

'I'm God, of course I'm preachy, it's part of the job.'

Peeper, never one for unnecessary confrontation pipes up in her chirpiest of voices, 'How about some lunch? Shall we have lunch? Isn't lunch nice?'

They all agree that lunch is—especially when compared to being shot at, fished by cannibals or lost in time—one of the nice things.

Chapter Seven

NEAL IS SITTING underneath the shade of an oak tree on the south point of Governors Island. He is doing what he always does: he is sketching in his large art pad, building worlds out of pencil and dreams. In those worlds, caped vigilantes haunt city streets capturing criminals; space policemen defend the world using the special powers conferred upon them by their alien employers; ancient spirits flit between host bodies, fighting crime long after death has stolen their own body away. When Neal dreams he dreams big. None of the superheroes and adventurers he sketches exist within the definitions most would use to classify reality. They are imagined figures. But this doesn't matter to Neal because he doesn't exist either, at least, not by those same limited definitions. Neal is the ghost of a young man who was once born here. He is a memory. A memory that continues to dream. And who are we to say that such dreams aren't just as real, just as important as anything else? There's certainly a lot of them living along this stretch of the Hudson.

As he shades the creamy blackness that lives beneath the cape of one of his heroes, he looks up and sees the Statue of Liberty turning to look at him.

Neal sighs and looks over towards Castle Williams where the Republican flag is being hoisted.

'Oh well,' he thinks, 'here we go again.'

Looks like it's going to be one of *those* days.

ON THE BANKS of Ellis Island, another ghost, young Annie Moore, also notices the Statue move. She rubs the gold, ten dollar coin they gave her when she first landed on these American shores, first off the boat from Ireland in 1892. It was a fortune to her then and now, haunting these shores as the fifteen year old she once was, it still sits in her coat pocket, heavy in her palm with the weight of opportunity. Today, once again someone is going to try to take it from her. She runs back to the dining hall to warn everyone that today is going to be a fighting day.

STANDING PROUD IN front of the ranks of Castle Williams' finest, General John Donald feels a warm glow in his troublesome belly. Often, this sort of intestinal action is a precursor to a violent explosion caused by canteen food. The General has a stomach that simply doesn't take to solids, but today he's fairly sure it's enthusiasm. After all, there is very little the General likes more than ordering a swarm of bullets into the flimsy, un-American bodies of the opposition.

'Gentlemen,' he says, looking down at the upturned faces of his troops, 'we are going to make this country great again.'

This is the sum total of his speech. His men don't need words to inspire them, that's what their wage is for. Besides, the light wind is playing havoc with his unruly hair; the straw-coloured flap of a comb-over is rising and falling like a drawbridge and he wants to fetch his cap so he can fix that son of a bitch in place.

'Sir?'

The General turns to his Colonel, a shrewd, slight man by the name of Heath Palin and experiences another strange feeling in that ever-shifting gastric system of his. *Fine looking man, Colonel Palin,* he thinks, *such a shame this damned war kept him from the love of a good wife.*

'Yes Colonel,' he replies, offering him what he hopes is a supportive, perhaps brotherly smile. 'What is it?'

Palin tries not to flinch at the sight of his General grimacing, his hair bowing towards him as if in genuflection. He loves his commanding officer, despite the fact that when he talks it's with a strained quality that suggests he's on the brink of a biologically hazardous bowel movement, but there's nothing quite so disturbing as the man's attempts at charm.

'A small boat has entered the field of combat sir,' Palin says. 'Probably nothing but I thought I should mention it.'

'Of course, Colonel,' the General nods and this brings the hair to a point of awful indecision, no longer at all sure in which direction it should be flicking. Colonel Palin stares deeply into his General's eyes, desperate not to look at the chaos going on a mere couple of inches above his pale yet explosive eyebrows. The General, deeply touched by the sudden, almost intimate attention being offered by his close subordinate, is suddenly desperate to take the man's hand and hold it for a short while. But that wouldn't look good in front of the rest of the troops. They might misunderstand what would be purely an act of comradeship for something more unpleasant, more un-American. Perhaps it's the fear of just such a misunderstanding that sees him suddenly, apropos of very little indeed, announce, 'I love beautiful women.'

Colonel Palin is slightly confused by this but does his best to nod as if this revelation was in some way relevant.

'I'm sure you do sir,' he replies, very much wishing they could all get on with the simple business of blowing holes in things.

'Yes, Colonel,' the General replies, 'and beautiful women love me. It has to go both ways.'

'I'm sure it does General, now, about that boat...'

'Indeed.' The General is returned to those few senses he possesses and he and Colonel Palin walk a short distance towards the high ridge around their camp and the coin-operated binoculars that are fixed there. Neither of the men has the slightest idea when the things were installed. This strange world they now find themselves in is an amalgam of centuries, objects, structures and people from all over the island's history. This includes themselves of course; they are the memories of other men from other times, they are flesh suits born of the land's dreaming. Not that they appreciate that fact; to do that would throw a considerable spanner into the worldview of both men and the soldiers enlisted beneath them. Sometimes, after a particularly long day shooting at things, both have questioned their existence slightly, wondered at the point of it all. Both put it down to an understandable sense of malaise caused by this "interminable goddamned war" and immediately brush the thoughts away. Philosophers will insist on questioning their place in the world, the rest of us have wisely decided the ineffable mysteries of creation are far easier to deal with if you simply ignore them. All the General and his men need to know is that Governors Island is their home and the undesirables are coming; the rest is gunpowder and rhetoric.

'Do you have a spare quarter, Colonel?' the General asks, holding out his hand in anticipation of the only answer he would expect from his second in command.

'I surely do, sir,' Colonel Palin replies, dropping one in the General's palm.

'You're a good man, Palin,' the General says as he tries to feed the coin into the slot on the binoculars, 'a very special man.'

'Thank you sir,' Colonel Palin reaches over and takes the coin from the General, 'allow me.' He turns the coin vertically rather than horizontally and drops it in.

'That's the way, Colonel.' The General looks out across the Hudson and soon finds the small boat in question. It is manned by the sort of people he'd really rather be looking at along the barrel of a musket than through a pair of binoculars.

'These are not good people, Colonel,' he says, 'these are not the sort of people we want in a decent, clean America.'

'No sir,' Colonel Palin agrees. 'I'm sure we can blow them out of the water along with all the rest of them.'

'That's the ticket, Colonel,' the General agrees. 'We will grind them beneath our firm, manly boots.' He looks momentarily confused and then disappointed. 'That is not the best metaphor, Colonel Palin because you cannot stand on water. I wish I had not said that. I am not a schmuck, let me tell you, I am a very smart guy.'

'Of course you are sir,' Colonel Palin agrees.

The General looks up into the sky, his hair lifting up as if his brain has flipped open its head hatch with the intention of leaving this sinking ship of a human being. 'What does a man do with water?' he wonders. 'He splashes it but that does not sound dramatic enough. I do not wish to splash that boat to death. I wish to do something more horrible than that.'

'Wreck, sir?' Colonel Palin suggests.

'Wreck, Colonel?'

'Well, it occurs to me that "wreck" is a suitably destructive naval term.'

The General nods, a smile creeping over his face. 'That it is, Colonel, that it is. Very well...' He clears his throat, all the better to orate with. 'We will wreck that boat and its passengers, Colonel, we shall wreck them to death.'

He nods, very pleased with himself.

Chapter Eight

On the *Baron Fabrizzi,* lunch is happening. It consists of some slightly damp bread, some hummus, pickles, processed cheese and a lot of potato chips, some of which are barbecue flavoured.

'This,' God announces, 'is a very good lunch. It is lunch operating at the very top of its game.'

'I'm glad you approve,' says Grace who is trying to make a sandwich out of absolutely everything.

'It's certainly a relief,' says Peeper, 'not to have anything trying to kill us for a few minutes.'

'Give it time,' says Demi-John while falling in love with hummus, a tasty thing he has not experienced before.

'That's life,' says God. 'Being attacked is the barbecue seasoning on the potato chip of existence. It makes things spicy.'

'Speak for yourself,' Grace replies. 'I'll happily spend

the rest of our journey being completely unspiced.'

'You say that now,' God tells her, holding up a piece of limp baguette, 'but remember how good this lunch tastes next time you have a boring morning followed by a mediocre meal.'

'Did the Statue of Liberty just smile at us?' Peeper asks.

'That's the thing with all experience,' God continues, ignoring Peeper completely, 'it's a matter of contrasts. Good things are better for having bad things happen around them. Nothing kills off enthusiasm better than monotony.'

'It definitely did,' says Peeper, 'a funny sort of smile. Kind of sad.'

'You didn't seem so enthusiastic when those men started shooting at us,' Grace says to God, a little tired of his putting a philosophical bent on things after the fact.

'Well,' he says, 'I'll admit I was a bit put out by that. Being machine-gunned is kind of dull, don't you think? I mean, compared to being attacked by Nazi U-Boats or cannibal fishermen. If I was still running things around here—which I'm not, this is all on you guys—I wouldn't have bothered with the machine gun stuff.'

'Does it matter how we end up dead?' she asked, finally losing her patience altogether. 'You're acting like this is all just fun. It's not to me, this is me trying to find my brother. Who may already be dead, and if he is, do you think I'll care if he died by a machine gun or a cannibal?'

'Well… no,' God admits. 'Sorry, I wasn't meaning to be insensitive. I just like to look on the bright side.'

'It's staring right down at us,' Peeper adds, as deaf to their conversation as they are to hers.

'You're right,' says Demi-John, because at least he's paying attention to his friend, 'she's definitely moving.'

'I hope she's not going to try and kill us,' says Peeper, 'like everything else has.'

'She looks too cheerful for that,' Demi-John replies.

'Depends if she enjoys killing things doesn't it?' Peeper points out. 'If she likes that kind of thing, the thought of doing it might put a smile on her face.'

'I suppose so.'

'What are you two talking about?' asks God, happy now to change the subject before he and Grace have a proper falling out.

'The Statue of Liberty,' Peeper explains, 'she's alive.'

Grace looks up. 'Oh,' she says.

'Oh,' agrees God, then adds a, 'Hello madam!' and a cheery wave, in the hope that the statue might respond to flattery.

'Maybe we should get out of here,' Grace decides, putting down the remains of her lunch and making for the engine controls, meaning to put themselves a polite distance away from the noble Libertas. 'We'll just get ourselves over towards Ellis island,' she says. 'It's probably hard work swimming if you're a massive statue.'

'I don't think you have to worry,' says God, 'look.'

The statue has hoisted its copper coated robes and is in the process of sitting down on her plinth. It takes a few awkward creaking seconds, but she ends up perched on the stone plinth, swinging her newly exposed legs and wafting her robes to create an updraft.

'I've never seen her legs before,' Demi-John admits.

'They ain't bad,' God adds.

'Are you two actually leering over a statue?' Grace asks.

'That would be ridiculous,' says God, 'I'm merely noting she's got a good set of gams on her. I mean it in a purely complimentary sense.'

'So do I,' says Demi-John, 'I'd gladly borrow them.'

'I'm sure she wouldn't be offended,' says God. 'I'll ask.

'Madam! Me and my friend Demi-John here have just been remarking on the quality of your legs.'

'Oh God…' Grace sighs.

'We meant no lasciviousness,' God continues.

'Definitely not!' Demi-John agrees, turning to Peeper. 'What's lasciviousness?'

'Sounds French, bound to be dirty,' Peeper replies.

'It was merely a passing observation given that we'd never noticed them before,' God finishes. 'I trust no offence was caused?'

The statue shrugs and waves the thought away nonchalantly.

'See?' says God. 'All is copacetic regarding the whole leg thing.'

Grace is staring at him, quite unable to believe how absurd her life has become.

'I don't suppose you'd fancy any lunch?' God shouts to the statue. 'It would be an honour to share it if you have a stomach to store it in?'

The statue smiles and shakes her head with the sound of a car crash that has been slowed down to a crawl. She then pats her stomach and there is a hollow echo.

'Fair enough,' says God. 'Well, we'll just finish ours and then head on our way.'

The statue slowly shakes her head, her face turning from a look of calm to concern. She points towards Governors Island and then pulls an exaggerated mime of fear, waving her hands.

'What does that that mean then?' Grace wonders.

The sound of a cannon cuts through the air as if in answer.

Dr Tom Hunterson sees Annie come running into the refectory, full of the news of an impending attack, and spares no time in ordering the alarm raised across the island. These repeated attacks from the crazy bastards at Castle Williams were really beginning to piss him off.

'Alright folks,' he says in his guttural, Kentucky accent,

words spilling out on top of one another as if desperate to escape his small, pinched mouth, 'looks like we've got ourselves a little bit of a conflict. Man the barricades, hoist the flags, stoke the flames and generally get your ass kicking boots strapped-on.'

Some would have described the citizens of Ellis Island as "dispossessed". It's a word that people that possess a lot like to use. In actuality they are, like their opposition on Governors Island, concepts grown solid. They are the ranks of all those who once set out from an old life in the hope of finding a new one here in America. They are immigrants, filling the cots and corridors of Ellis Island's official buildings. They are dreamers.

'General Donald wants to clean us off his precious shores,' says Hunterson. 'As always he's welcome to try.'

Chapter Nine

THE GENERAL IS somewhat put out. Whenever he gives the order for the cannon to be fired—the clarion call of God's Righteousness (*let it ring out like the trumpets of heaven, hallelujah*)—the sudden noise always makes him jump. Every Goddamned Time. He knows that Colonel Palin notices, though the wonderful man would never point it out, and it embarrasses him rotten. As always, he feels the only way to compensate for any temporary loss to his masculinity is to bring out the fire and brimstone.

'Men!' he shouts. 'Let this be the deciding day in our holy crusade, let this be the day that virtue finally stamps out the pests in our nests!'

He is so impressed by that last rhyming phrase he quite runs out of words and finishes his speech by simply waving his arms, nodding a lot and punching at the air. If the men are disappointed in this slightly comical dumb show they give no sign of it. They offer up a—in all honesty, a rather tired and lacklustre—cheer and then wander towards their posts.

'Today will be the day, Colonel,' says the General, 'no more half measures. Today we will wipe them out to a man.' He smiles. 'You've got to think big, Colonel, I mean, you have to think anyway, so why not think big?'

'Wise words, sir,' Colonel Palin replies.

The General nods, Colonel Palin isn't telling him anything he doesn't already know.

On Ellis Island, Doc Hunterson's informal band of soldiers splits off along the shore, running to man the island's eclectic array of weapon posts. Ancient cannon, machine gun nests, even an absurd, jerry-rigged catapult constructed by an enthusiastic band of Norwegians, perhaps seeking to channel their ancient Viking heritage— all are occupied, prepared for action.

'Don't wait on my account,' shouts Doc Hunterson through a battered bullhorn. 'You'll get no bonus points for politeness. Fire at will!'

'This isn't our war!' screams Demi-John, as the air begins to fill with the unwelcome presence of heavy artillery. He's not the first young man to shout something similar in the incendiary history of this country's love affair with violence. His plea for neutrality goes just as unheard as all before him.

'We need to move!' Grace shouts, just as a cannonball hits the water only a few feet away, showering them in spray.

'I don't like the idea of trying to cruise through that,' says God, 'and if we go back…'

'We'll meet the nasty men with the loud guns again,' Peeper finishes for him. 'You think this is why they turned around when they were chasing us?'

'For sure,' Grace agrees. 'They knew this part of the river was a killer.'

'We can't just stay here either,' pleads Demi-John as another cannon ball narrowly misses them.

'Maybe we should make for land,' suggests Grace, 'but which side? For all we know either army might shoot us dead on the spot.'

'Mr Monitor?' asks Gracie Fforde. 'Would you be so good as to top up my glass?'

'Of course,' he agrees, gently pouring his employer another measure of syrupy frozen vodka before replacing the bottle in their portable icebox.

'I do love a good war,' she says, relaxing into her deckchair.

'Indeed ma'am,' Monitor agrees, 'it's a perfect way to let the hair down after a frustrating morning.'

'Exactly that,' she agrees. 'Mr Monitor there are times when I really think we are of one mind.'

'You flatter me,' he replies with a subservient bow. Never let your employer see you as too dominant, it always brings out their most vicious, defensive qualities.

'Yes,' she nods, 'perhaps I do. Oh well, don't let it go to your head.'

'Never, ma'am.'

MANY BOOKS HAVE been written about the art of war, imbuing it with a sharp, cerebral intelligence. A game of strategy where each piece to fall is a human life. Such books are extremely popular amongst soldiers of rank; after all, they're rarely the ones doing the screaming in agony. This is not to say that war cannot be skilful, tacticians the world over have found success by using their head as well as their fists. Ultimately though, this sort of battle is in the minority, especially in the modern age, and the problem with consistently thinking of war in such intellectual terms is that it exaggerates the cerebral while underestimating the physical. For every master campaigner, every truly gifted leader, there are countless homicidal bunglers. Most war is not clever. Most war is just people bleeding all over the place.

War is a numbers game and is conventionally won on two very basic principles: who has the biggest weapons and who possesses the most soldiers. You might be leading the most skilled ninja warriors the world has ever seen, a clan of weaponised human beings whose skills in combat are awesome to see, the sort of lithe, kung-fu legends that can kill an opponent simply by breathing on them. If the other side drops a dirty great thermonuclear device on them though, their skills are worthless. You cannot defeat a warhead on the field of battle using martial arts. Missiles care little whether you punch them on the nose. Likewise, an entire tribe of dedicated, spear-carrying tribesmen will always struggle when faced with a slew of tanks. Extending these principles to their logical conclusion, if you want to win a war then all you really need is enough money to horrendously overcompensate with your weaponry and a cold lump of ice where your heart should be.

This war is different. Both sides are ill-equipped, disorganised and a wee bit mental.

The battle is fought like this: both sides hurl absolutely everything they have at one another and hope for the best. As methods of combat go it scores highly in enthusiasm but loses points for efficacy.

On the banks of Governors Island, an enthusiastic young soldier cheers as he manages to hit an old man square on the chest with an ancient munitions shell. The shell sails through the old man, leaving a bone-framed window behind, then explodes on impact with the ground behind him, killing nobody else. A cannon ball from Ellis Island lands on the briefly triumphant young soldier's head and reduces it to a fine mist. Two casualties brought down by weapons that were designed to be more than overweight bullets. Not only is it a horrible waste of life (or at least what passes for life amongst these semi-imaginary combatants, both old man and young soldier will be back to fight again another day) it is a horrible waste of ammunition.

The ad hoc catapult on Ellis Island begins the battle by flinging rocks and bits of masonry. After a while, once supplies of both have run dry, it is flinging kitchen equipment. A saucepan, if travelling fast enough, will kill someone just as effectively as a brick—albeit with a much more impressive sound on impact—but you really do need to take a long hard look at your war once it's relying on raiding kitchen cupboards to achieve success.

Not that all of the weapons posts can be said to be so lacking. A machine gun nest, operated by a normally rather shy and uncertain lady from Poland, is achieving great things as it cuts a band of churned grass and churned bodies along the coast of Governors Island. In fact, were it not for a lucky shot on the part of Colonel Heath Palin as one of his rifle bullets ricochets off the howitzer housing and hits the Polish lady right on the nose, she might have won the day's battle for Ellis Island all on her own.

* * *

'HAVE WE WRECKED that little boat yet, Colonel?' the General asks.

'Sadly not, sir,' the Colonel replies, 'though I'm sure it's only a matter of time.'

'What are they doing? Are they returning fire?'

'No sir, as far as I can see they're just sitting there on the edge of the combat area.'

'Lazy,' says the General, shaking his head as if deeply saddened by this news. 'I shouldn't be surprised, laziness is a trait in blacks.'

'If you say so sir.'

'I do, I do. They are a passionless people. Without passion you don't have energy, without energy you have nothing.'

Colonel Palin wonders if it's necessary to agree to this as well but realises his General isn't really listening anymore. He's staring into space, his lips moving slightly as he orates speeches in the empty halls of his own mind.

Colonel Palin decides it is best to leave his superior to this somewhat distracted behaviour; he has an idea how to bring the man's thoughts into focus.

'I THINK YOU should go for Ellis Island,' God suggests.

'OK,' Grace agrees, gunning the engine and making for

the southern side of the island, hoping to avoid bringing them directly into the cross fire.

It's the best of a limited set of potentially fatal options and it's such a shame that it ends the way it does.

Chapter Ten

COLONEL PALIN TAPS Lieutenant Hicks on the shoulder. Hicks is a good man and has killed a lot of people over the long weeks of this interminable campaign.

'Move aside for a moment, soldier,' Palin tells him.

Hicks may be saddened to pause in his gleeful of duty of turning the enemy into hamburger meat but is enough of a professional not to let it show. 'Sir,' he replies, nodding and stepping back.

Palin takes the controls of the howitzer and sets his sights on the *Baron Fabrizzi*. It's now on the move but Palin doesn't mind that, quite the reverse in fact, if it had been a completely static target he would have felt shooting it bordered on the dishonourable. He does his best to compensate for the boat's speed and direction and then lets the shell fly.

*   *   *

THE *BARON FABRIZZI* is close to shore when the shell bores through it, both tipping and splitting the vessel. Its lack of explosive charge is some compensation, though it's something that will occur to the crew only later. At the moment of impact, flung into the water and surrounded by the shrapnel of impact, none of them have due cause for a single positive thought.

PALIN ALLOWS HICKS to return to his post and returns to his General's side to impart the good news.

'The small boat has been hit, sir,' he says. 'I saw to it myself. I reduced it to matchwood with a single shell.'

When the General looks at his Colonel, it is with tears in his puffy, poisonous and piggy little eyes. Palin is pleased, then momentarily concerned as he's convinced the old man means to kiss him. Thankfully, the momentary urge seems to pass and the General settles for grabbing him in a bear hug. 'You're a wonderful man, Colonel Palin,' he says, balling his pink little hands in the Colonel's back. 'Right now, Jesus is making plans as to how to honour you the minute you enter His Glorious Kingdom.'

'Thank you sir.'

'I would not be at all surprised if it involves some form of throne,' the General continues, 'a really nice one with gold trimming. Maybe even some form of honorary title. Do you think they have honorary titles in heaven, Colonel?'

'I couldn't say sir,' Palin answers honestly, he has become distracted by something pressing into his hip. He supposes it must be the General's revolver, slung on the man's belt. Yes, that will certainly be what this thing is that seems to be nudging at him like a small puppy forcing itself into the soft flesh of its mother's belly.

'Sir?' he asks, aware that they should really be returning to the battle.

'Yes, Colonel?' the General says and Colonel Palin is aware that the man is rubbing his cheek on his shoulder.

'I must return to my post, sir,' Colonel Palin says.

'Indeed you must,' the General agrees, slowly, reluctantly, letting go of his subordinate. 'To continue the good work.'

'Yes sir.' Colonel Palin gives his General a brief salute, ignoring the contorted way his superior seems to be standing, tugging at the hem of his uniform jacket and fiddling with his belt and holster as if trying to get it to sit properly.

'Give them one from me, Colonel,' the General says. 'I must attend to a call of nature.'

FOR GRACE THE world is one of light and sound, of rushing air that beats at her with sharp, wooden teeth, then she's in the water and, for a moment, she knows nothing. It's like night has fallen hard enough to concuss.

The gap in awareness is then replaced with a mighty pressure and the distorted sound of the explosions above, filtered through the thick cushion of the river water. She opens her eyes but she can't see anything in the murky green and brown world around her. Her senses are useless, distorted roaring and bubbling, no concept of up or down, just a new world she can no longer live in. She's breathed in water and it's making her choke but each convulsion of her lungs makes the situation worse and it's getting darker as, right on the periphery of her attention, she's aware of something large moving towards her. Then perception's gone again.

The next thing she knows she's surrounded by light and air, throwing up river water as the earth of Ellis Island looms before her and she's dropped, face down into the dirt.

There's a coughing from somewhere nearby and she lifts her head from the regurgitated contents of her own sorry stomach to see Demi-John lying next to her. He's looking as disorientated as she feels, flailing in the mud and looking up at the sky behind them.

She wonders what he's looking at. In a minute she'll take a look, she decides. Yes, in a minute, when her stomach stops churning.

The water splashes behind her and she hears God shouting.

'Peeper!' he's shouting. 'Never mind me! Peeper!'

The panic in his voice shakes some clarity into Grace and she turns to see the Statue of Liberty. She's dropped her stone tablet and is now carrying God instead, her other hand still carries the torch which she's using to bat away munitions fire. The forces of Governors Island can't resist such a target and, for a moment, they're all aiming at her.

'Peeper!' God shouts. 'She's still in the water! Find Peeper!'

Grace looks at the water, trying to see any sign of the girl in the crush of the waves and the debris of their boat.

The statue drops God to the earth and turns back to continue the search.

God's false beard is parted and Pam's small face pokes out, squirting river water from her pouting mouth. She's the living embodiment of the sort of water feature tasteless people buy to enliven tacky modern houses.

Demi-John is dragging himself towards the water's edge, meaning to dive back in and help the statue search for his friend. Grace grabs him.

'You're a lousy swimmer,' she reminds him. 'You get to higher ground and be a lookout for her.'

'She won't die?' he asks, as if it's a question Grace can possibly answer. 'That's not going to happen is it?'

'Not while we can help it,' she tells him, because it's the most honest answer she can bear to give. She turns back towards the river, ducking as a hail of bullets ricochets off the statue. Libertas doesn't care, just wades back towards the deeper water, stooping down to rake through the river with her huge fingers.

She finds nothing.

THE STATUE OF Liberty's decision to come down off her pedestal and enter the action does not go unremarked upon. On Governors Island, the General is incensed.

'That metal woman is disgusting!' he shouts. 'Both inside and out. How dare she take sides like this?'

His anger is so intense that his stomach, rebellious at the best of times, becomes a positive riot of gaseous indignation. Luckily for him, and the sensibilities of his men, the sound of the guns covers his own explosive barrage.

'Slap that bitch silly!' he cries only half aware of the terrible things occurring behind the draped curtains of his tailcoat. 'It's time she was put back in her place.'

On Ellis Island, unsurprisingly, the feelings towards Libertas err towards the positive.

'About time she rolled up her sleeves and stepped in,' says Doc Hunterson. 'Mind you, she's taken a beating over the years, can't blame her for washing her hands of us I guess.' Meanwhile, further away, it's not the statue that's drawn an enthusiastic response, rather the sinking of the *Baron Fabrizzi*.

'Oh that was brilliant!' cries Gracie Fforde, spilling her drink slightly as she claps her hands in excitement. 'Much better than if my Coast Guard had shot them.'

'More dramatic,' Mr Monitor agrees.

'I wonder though,' says Fforde, 'if we're not failing in our duty as citizens of this new America.'

'How so ma'am?'

'Sitting here as bystanders, Mr Monitor. I think we should do our bit.' She drains her drink and hands him her glass. 'I'm sure we brought a few toys didn't we?'

Mr Monitor is now aware the direction in which his employer's mind is turning. 'We did, ma'am.'

Fforde moves over to their car and pops the trunk, her eyes lighting up as she sees what's inside. 'Oh my God, *yes*, that's just what we need.'

Chapter Eleven

UNAWARE OF THE fact they've drawn an audience and far too concerned with finding their lost friend, Grace, God, Demi-John and the statue have no idea of the dangerous attention homing in on them.

The combatting armies have once again turned to one another, ignoring the little drama that's playing out on the periphery. They have a dwindling supply of munitions to hurl at one another and they're eager to get on with the business of hurling them.

'Where is she?' God is shouting and Grace has never seen him so shaken. The façade he always wears, of the omniscient, unshakeable deity has dropped. Now he's just a fragile, middle-aged man desperate to avoid the horrible possibility that he has just lost a friend. 'She can't stay underwater this long, she just can't!'

Grace looks up towards Demi-John, dragging himself

along, trying to find a vantage point where he might be able to see Peeper. His face is slack, in shock, in denial. He is closer to her than any of them; they grew up together in the uncomfortable attention of fairground audiences, consoling one another, supporting one another. For a moment she feels a terrible sense of responsibility. She shouldn't have let either of them come with her on this crazy journey. She didn't force them, the choice was theirs, but if they'd stayed back in Coney Island they'd both have been safer and probably happier.

The Statue of Liberty stands up straight and turns to look towards them, her face creaking into a sad frown.

'Keep looking!' God shouts. Then starts wading in. 'Fine, leave it to me, I'll get her...' He pulls Pam from his beard. 'You could help!'

Then there's a surge of water, several metres away, white froth and a giant shape pushing its way up into the air. It's Kipsy and on her back, hanging on for dear life, Peeper. Kipsy gives a bark of greeting and pushes her way towards the shoreline, keeping low and out of the range of the crossfire.

'Kipsy!' Grace shouts, jumping up and down with just the sort of unrestrained happiness she had pretty much given up on feeling years ago. Behind her, she can hear Demi-John laughing and clapping and God is spinning around on the spot, holding Pam by her feet so she spins along with him, giggling at the madness of it all.

Then there is a loud whooshing sound and the Statue of Liberty's back explodes in a burst of flame.

'THAT'S WHAT I'M talking about,' says Gracie Fforde, lowering the RPG from her shoulder. 'One in the ass for the libertarians!'

'Perfect shot, ma'am,' Mr Monitor agrees.

'Pass me another grenade,' Fforde asks.

KIPSY VIRTUALLY GLIDES onto the land; Peeper, breathless, dazed but safe, slipping from her back and onto the grass.

Behind them, the Statue of Liberty is reeling, her chest is swollen and split and, as she turns towards the direction of her attackers, all can see the gaping wound in her back.

Another grenade streaks towards her but she's ready for this one, slugging it with her torch like a baseball batsman looking to drive his entire team home.

'OH,' SAYS GRACIE Fforde, 'that's not meant to happen.'

THE GRENADE HITS the shore of Governors Island where it takes out two gun placements and sends three soldiers sailing through the air. The tide was beginning to turn against the General's men, anyway, as their conventional munitions ran dry against the more eclectic weaponry of the opposition. This is a deciding strike and even the General, in his own stupid way, knows it.

'Colonel Palin,' he says, 'I am giving serious consideration to calling a retreat.'

'Yes sir?'

'Oh indeed yes. I know it stands against everything we believe in but, in war, one must look to the long game. Sometimes by losing a battle you can win the war.'

'Yes sir?' Palin, who has just seen another of his men decapitated by a catapulted office chair, is wishing his General would stop orating and just call this mess quits.

'Certainly, Colonel. Part of being a winner is knowing when enough is enough. Sometimes you have to give up the fight and walk away. Move on to something more productive.'

'Shall I give the order sir?' the Colonel asks, his impatience noticeable.

'The men deserve to hear it from me,' the General announces. 'Stand aside.'

ON ELLIS ISLAND, Doc Hunterson's troops are also at the point of giving up. He looks around and can see little but destruction and dead bodies. *Goddamnit*, he thinks, *but there has to be a better way of getting on in life than this. This hoopla just ain't getting anyone anywhere.* Then he sees the tiny figure of the distant General, standing up to speak to his troops.

Well, OK then, Doc thinks, *maybe just one more little volley.* He runs towards the catapult. 'What have you got left to throw at them boys?' he asks the Norwegians.

'Not so much,' one admits, a young man by the name of Alf. 'I was about to start loading the crockery.'

Doc Hunterson selects a large serving plate and hands it over to one of Alf's colleagues. 'A parting gift for the General,' he suggests, nodding towards Governors Island.

'MEN!' THE GENERAL calls. 'It is time we face facts. Sometimes you have to learn from the past, which is what we call history, and follow the lessons it teaches us.'

Oh just get on with it! Colonel Palin is thinking. *While we still have a few men alive enough to hear you.*

A swirl of wind lifts the Governor's combover into an epic, almost Lovecraftian, swarm of blonde and grey above his orange, strained face. He wonders whether he should try to straighten it before continuing. Certainly a couple of his remaining troops seem deeply disturbed by the sight of it. He doesn't want them to miss the beauty of his words, distracted by the unfortunate follicle rebellion occurring above.

'A moment,' he announces, reaching for the comb in his jacket, 'I shall just deal with this.'

There's no need, a heavy china serving plate deals with it for him as it hits him in his sagging throat. His head leaves his body, tumbling onto the plate where it flies a few more feet, a startled pig's head waiting for a decorative apple to be crammed in its sewer-like mouth before coming to land, miraculously intact, on the grass several feet away.

Hiding in the trees, the ghost of young Neal laughs and does a quick sketch of it in his notepad so as to preserve the moment for posterity.

The General's body, slow on the uptake with regards what's going on above its neckerchief, issues a long, almost triumphant fart, a trumpet declaring the retreat and then topples back into the dirt, squashing out its final, muffled note against the churned up earth.

'Retreat!' Colonel Palin screams, and he leads by example, he and his men running hell for leather back to the comparative safety of Castle Williams.

'WELL,' SAYS DOC Hunterson, 'I guess that's just about all she wrote for today then. Let's look to getting some of this mess tidied up.'

And with that, a war is done for the day.

Well, *almost*...

*   *   *

'ANOTHER GRENADE!' GRACIE Fforde is shouting. 'Quickly man, I'll teach that uppity skank how we do things these days.'

Mr Monitor is feeling something he hasn't felt for some considerable time: concern. He is far from content with his employer's track record today and while he knows he should count it as a momentary glitch on the continued path to comfortable living, her panicked, chaotic manner is offending him. Part of the reason he has always had confidence in Ms Fforde's ability to surf the apocalyptic waves post-Change is her sheer unflappability. This shrieking, incensed woman is not quite as reassuring. After a fraction of a second's consideration he hands her the grenade nonetheless but he also takes a few more steps back than are strictly speaking necessary for safe firing clearance. Those steps are instinctual. Later, when he takes a moment to consider them, he will wonder what prompted him to act in such a way, how could he have known what was to come? He won't find a satisfactory answer. Neither will he really care, by then he will be far too happy, having taken over his employer's company and place in The Hellfire Club, to let such minor niggles clutter up his head.

'"Give me your tired,"' Grace is muttering as she loads

the RPG, '"your poor, your huddled masses"...' the grenade locks into place, 'and I'll give them a one way ticket out of this fine damned country of ours.'

She does not notice the shadow falling over her as she concentrates on the RPG. Mr Monitor does and begins to run.

By the time Ms Fforde is aware that all is not well in her world, that the irritations of the day have been nothing but minor blips compared to what is to come, it is far too late for her to do anything about it.

She has time only to register that the large shape falling towards her is the Statue of Liberty's torch, the briefest of moments to be irritated at the symbolism of it all, and then she is reduced to a sort of gritty paste beneath nine metres of gold-plate, copper, stone and history.

'SORRY ABOUT THE torch,' says Grace as the Statue of Liberty wades across the Hudson. The statue affects a sort of shrug, lifting her hands as high above her head as possible as she crosses the deepest part of the river so as to keep the people sat in them safe.

'I miss our boat,' says God, leaning casually against a thumb. Pam is plaiting his false beard for him. 'It was a very nice boat.'

'I'll miss Kipsy more,' says Peeper, waving at the creature as she swims south, heading back out to deeper waters.

'At least none of us has to miss you,' Demi-John points out, giving her a hug.

The statue places them gently on the quayside at Battery Park, looks at God, blows him a kiss, winks and then wades back to her island.

'What a woman,' he sighs, then chases after Pam who is running towards the trees and the park itself.

'I am sorry about the boat really,' Peeper tells Grace. 'I know it would have been easier to get to where your brother might be if we'd stayed on the river.'

Grace shrugs. 'Who knows? Easy hasn't really come into it so far.'

And deep down, she knows it never will.